Princess Poppy

The Tooth Fairy

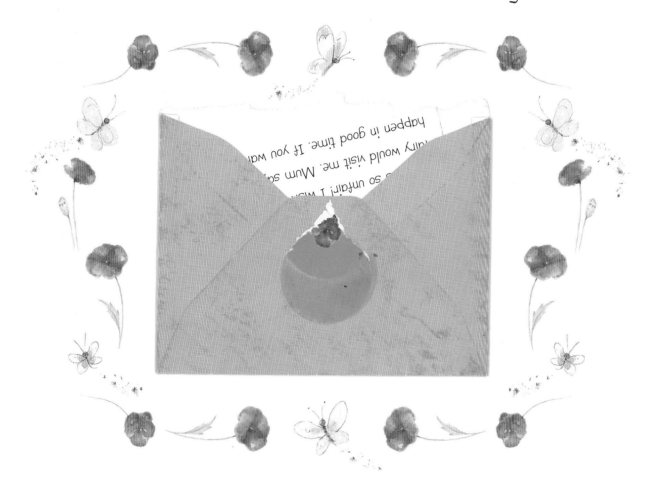

Written by **Janey Louise Jones**

PICTURE CORGI

Check out Princess Poppy's brilliant website:

★

www.princesspoppy.com

With love for Isla Rose,
a little princess

THE TOOTH FAIRY
A PICTURE CORGI BOOK 978 0 552 56151 8

Published in Great Britain by Picture Corgi,
an imprint of Random House Children's Books
A Random House Group Company

This edition published 2010

1 3 5 7 9 10 8 6 4 2

Text copyright © Janey Louise Jones, 2010
Illustrations copyright © Picture Corgi Books, 2010
Illustrations by Veronica Vasylenko
Design by Tracey Cunnell

The right of Janey Louise Jones and Veronica Vasylenko to be identified as the author and illustrator
of this work has been asserted in accordance with the Copyright, Designs and Patents Act 1988.

RANDOM HOUSE CHILDREN'S BOOKS
61-63 Uxbridge Road, London W5 5SA

www.kidsatrandomhouse.co.uk
www.princesspoppy.com
www.rbooks.co.uk

Addresses for companies within The Random House Group Limited
can be found at: www.randomhouse.co.uk/offices.htm

THE RANDOM HOUSE GROUP Limited Reg. No. 954009

A CIP catalogue record for this book is available from the British Library.

Printed in China

The Tooth Fairy

featuring

Mum
★

Princess Poppy
★

Grandpa
★

Honey
★

The tooth fairy
★

"Everyone in my class has lost at least one tooth *and* been visited by the tooth fairy," complained Poppy. "None of mine are even wobbly yet. It's so unfair!"

"It'll happen, darling," smiled Grandpa. "You just have to be patient."

Humph, thought Poppy. She didn't like waiting for things.

Every morning Poppy checked each tooth in turn.

Every night she did the very same thing, and when none of them were wobbly she always felt a sting of disappointment.

Poppy was longing for a visit from the tooth fairy.

One Friday Poppy arrived at school to find her friends chatting excitedly.

"The tooth fairy visited me again last night!" squealed Mimosa with a gappy grin. "And guess what? I saw her fly away through my window. She was beautiful! She looks just like the fairy from the top of the Christmas tree – all golden and sparkly."

"Wow!" said Honey. "I wish I had seen her when she came to visit me last week."

"I'm going to stay awake all night next time so that I see her," declared Sweetpea.

"Me too!" said Abigail.

Poppy felt very left out indeed and decided that she would have to do something to make her teeth wobble.

On Saturday, Mum and Dad took Poppy, Honey and the twins to the Camomile Cove Fun Fair. Usually Poppy would have been super excited, but all she could think about was the tooth fairy.

When they arrived, Poppy spotted the toffee apple stall, which gave her an idea.

She ran over, bought herself one and bit into the delicious treat. It was very hard and crunchy and Poppy was certain that one of her teeth had moved.

She grabbed Honey's hand and ran to the Magic Hall of Mirrors to have a look . . .

First she tried to push the tooth
with her tongue, willing it to move . . .

Then she tried to wobble
it with her fingers . . .

But to Poppy's disappointment the tooth was still rock solid in her gum.
"I will have baby teeth for ever and I'll never get a visit from the tooth
fairy!" she sobbed. "It's so unfair!"

Honey gave her best friend a hug.

"Don't worry, Poppy. I just know it will happen really soon!"

All the way home Poppy felt miserable. Why were none of her teeth wobbly yet?

That Sunday, during lunch, Poppy chewed on her roast beef and crispy roast potatoes with extra might in the hope that it would help. But it was no good. Not a single tooth budged. Even the sticky fudge pudding did nothing.

The next day, to cheer Poppy up, Mum collected her from school and took her and her friends to Bumble Bee's Teashop for a hot chocolate with whippy cream and one of Granny Bumble's delicious home-made biscuits.

When Poppy bit into her wholemeal fruit and nut biscuit she felt something strange. She took another bite, chewing her mouthful carefully. This time she was sure that one of her teeth had moved . . .

"Honey!" she whispered, worried that it might turn out to be another false alarm.
"I think I've got a wobbler!"

"Wow!" said Honey, as she peered at the tooth. "It's *definitely* loose!
Everyone, Poppy's got a wobbly tooth!"

"Yippee! I'm going to see the tooth fairy!" declared Poppy.

Poppy could hardly contain her excitement, but she hadn't thought about the long
wait ahead. Although the tooth was wobbly it was still strongly attached to her gum.

She tried to make the time pass faster by imagining
what the tooth fairy might look like . . .

Does she have sparkly wings?

Does she have fairy helpers?

Does she have long flowing hair?

Does she live in a castle?

Does she leave a magical trail?

Does she play with butterflies?

Does she wear pretty shoes?

After two weeks of having a wobbly tooth Poppy began to get worried that it would never happen.

"Muuuum," she whinged, one day after school, "I don't think my tooth is ever going to come out. Sweetpea's tooth got wobbly way after mine and it's fallen out already!"

"Don't worry, sweetheart," smiled Mum. "These things take time and everybody is different. You know how the baby swans on Peppermint Pond had downy baby coats for ages and now their elegant and graceful grown-up feathers have come? That's just like your teeth – they'll appear when they're good and ready."

The next morning, when Poppy had almost given up hope, she bit into her toast and, with a **wibble,**

a wobble

and a pop, out her tooth came!

"Yippee, the fairy will come tonight!" she exclaimed gleefully, holding the tooth up for her family to see.

After breakfast, Poppy brushed her teeth and then ran all the way to school, desperate to tell her friends the exciting news.

Eventually, after the slowest day ever, the evening came. Usually Poppy did anything she could to stay up past her bed time, but that night she couldn't wait to go to bed.

She put her tooth in a silk bag and slipped it under her pillow, feeling as excited as if it were the night before her birthday.

"I won't sleep a wink," she declared.

"The tooth fairy won't come if you're awake," replied Mum. "She's very shy."

But Poppy was desperate to catch a glimpse of a real fairy . . .

When Poppy awoke at dawn, disappointed that she'd not managed to stay awake, she lifted her pillow to find a silver coin and no tooth!

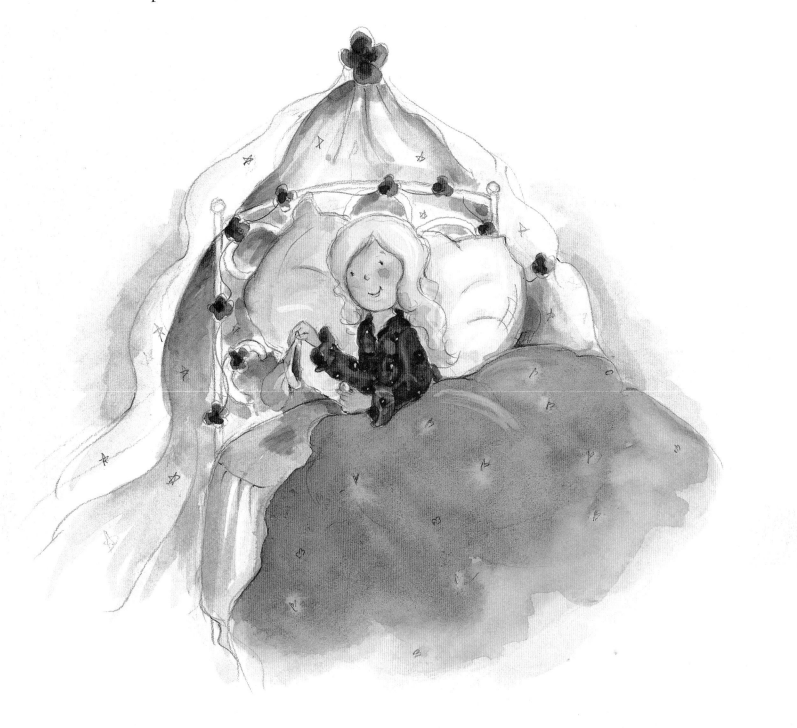

She ran to the window in the hope of seeing the tooth fairy flying away, but there was nothing . . .

or was that a trail of sparkling fairy dust?

"Mum! She's been!" called Poppy.

"Did you see her, darling?" asked Mum.

"No, but I think I know what the tooth fairy does with all the teeth," replied Poppy. "She turns them into magical fairy dust to give her special powers!"

Mum smiled. "My patient little gap-toothed princess!"